Freddie visits the dentist

Nicola Smee

Bear's never been to the dentist,
so he's coming with me for a check-up.

Hello Freddie!

I show Bear the dentist's chair which he can move up and down like a see-saw!

That should be high enough, Freddie!

I open my mouth very wide for the dentist to check my teeth. It doesn't hurt at all!

What's that funny, red, wiggly thing?

"Now I'm going to give your teeth a polish," says the dentist. "This will tickle a little!"

“Well done, Freddie. Your teeth are sparkling and clean,” says the dentist. “Now let’s have a look at Bear.”

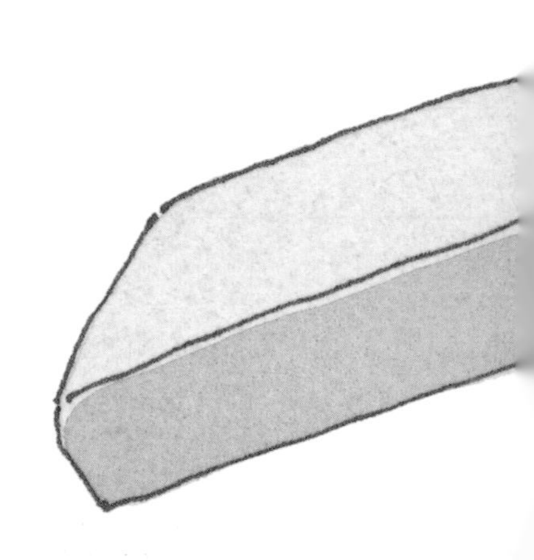

But I don't have any teeth !

"Never mind, Bear," I say. "Have a rinse with this nice pink water."

When we leave, the dentist gives me a new toothbrush. Bear says HE wants one as well!

Remember Freddie, not too many sweets !

I must keep my teeth
brushed and clean,
the way the dentist showed me!